PREPARING FOR DISASTER™

ENGINEERING SOLUTIONS FOR HURRICANES

JERI FREEDMAN

New York

Published in 2020 by The Rosen Publishing Group, Inc.
29 East 21st Street, New York, NY 10010

First Edition

Library of Congress Cataloging-in-Publication Data

Names: Freedman, Jeri, author.
Title: Engineering solutions for hurricanes / Jeri Freedman.
Description: First edition. | New York: Rosen Publishing, 2020. | Series: Preparing for disaster | Audience: Grades 5 to 8. | Includes bibliographical references and index.
Identifiers: LCCN 2019009984| ISBN 9781725347854 (library bound) | ISBN 9781725347847 (pbk.)
Subjects: LCSH: Hurricanes—Juvenile literature. | Hurricane protection—Juvenile literature. | Hazard mitigation—Juvenile literature. | Emergency management—Juvenile literature.
Classification: LCC QC944.2 .F74 2020 | DDC 363.34/922—dc23
LC record available at https://lccn.loc.gov/2019009984

Manufactured in the United States of America

CONTENTS

Introduction

Hurricanes are spinning storms with extreme winds and rain. They are called hurricanes in the Atlantic and northwest Pacific Oceans, cyclones in the South Pacific and Indian Oceans, and typhoons in the western Pacific. The biggest recorded hurricane was the 1979 Pacific hurricane called Typhoon Tip. It had a diameter of around 1,380 miles (2,220 kilometers). Most hurricanes form and remain at sea. When they travel toward land, though, they can cause horrible damage. They can produce winds up to 175 miles per hour (282 kilometers per hour). They bring massive flooding from heavy rains. They can also cause storm surges (risings of the sea) as high as 20 feet (6 meters) that extend at the extreme end of the range to more than 93 miles (150 km).

In 2005, Hurricane Katrina struck Louisiana and other states around the Gulf of Mexico. It killed more than 1,800 people in the United States and caused more than $161 billion in property damage, according to the Office of Coastal Management, a part of the National Oceanic and Atmospheric Administration (NOAA). Hardest hit was the city of New Orleans, which was flooded when poorly designed levees around Lake Pontchartrain gave way. The experience of New Orleans—and other cities that have been destroyed by hurricanes—shows how important proper engineering is for creating structures that can withstand such extreme storms. This job is not an easy task.

Science, technology, engineering, and mathematics (STEM) are subjects that provide the knowledge and skills to solve hurricane-related problems. Scientists are

Water pours over a failing levee, flooding the city of New Orleans, Louisiana, during Hurricane Katrina in 2005.

studying how hurricanes form to forecast when and where they will strike. They are also working to better understand the features and behavior of hurricanes. They need this knowledge because hurricanes have been becoming stronger in response to global climate change. Engineers are working with state and local governments to develop building codes for structures that will better survive hurricanes. They are producing improved designs and standards for buildings, water drainage systems, and other key features of cities to protect communities in hurricane zones. Engineers must engage with governments and the private sector to ensure that structures in these areas are better located, planned, designed, and built.

CHAPTER ONE

Mighty Storms

Hurricanes are also called tropical cyclones. The term "cyclone," from a Greek word for "circle," refers to a windstorm that spins. This spinning is called rotation. Hurricanes rotate in a counterclockwise direction in the Northern Hemisphere and clockwise in the Southern Hemisphere. Most hurricanes form in the tropics, the area of Earth surrounding the equator. They most commonly develop in the tropical part of the Atlantic Ocean, the Caribbean Sea, and the Gulf of Mexico. Hurricanes start with a tropical depression. A tropical depression is an area of low pressure in the tropics that causes a rotating group of thunderstorms with winds of less than 39 miles per hour (62 kmh). When the winds reach 39 to 73 miles per hour (63–117.5 kmh), the tropical depression becomes a tropical storm. When winds reach 74 miles per hour (118 kmh), they are classified as a hurricane.

Hurricanes can cause massive damage to property and injure and kill people. Their destructive effects are the result of heavy rain, flooding, storm surges, and powerful winds. Hurricanes are measured by the Saffir-Simpson Hurricane Wind Scale. This scale rates them as category 1 to 5, according to a hurricane's maximum sustained winds. The higher a hurricane's category, the greater its potential for damage. The hurricane season runs from

Powerful hurricane winds tear a sign from its frame and send it crashing into a building during Hurricane Harvey in 2017.

June 1 to November 30, although hurricanes occasionally occur outside this period.

The World Meteorological Organization (WMO) names hurricanes alphabetically, starting with *A*. The WMO starts with a list of people's names that is to be used for each year. After six years, the WMO reuses the list of names. (For example, in 2020, the same list of names is used again in 2026.) When a hurricane causes great damage, its name is retired. The names Andrew, Katrina, Harvey, and Maria have been retired. The WMO chooses another name to replace a name that has been retired.

How a Hurricane Forms

Hurricanes form in areas where ocean water is warm, humidity is high, and winds are light. They need water that is at least 80 degrees Fahrenheit (27 degrees Celsius) to a depth of at least 150 feet (45 m). When the hot air rises and meets cold air, the result is a tropical thunderstorm, which may become a hurricane. The air must be humid (filled with water), which adds fuel to the storm. Many tropical storms and hurricanes begin when stormy weather in Africa moves into the ocean by the Cape Verde Islands and proceeds west into the Atlantic Ocean.

One of the most notable features of hurricanes is their spinning, which generates powerful winds. The source of their spin is the Coriolis force, which is generated by Earth's rotation. It spins a moving storm much like a toy top. The Coriolis force is zero at the equator (an imaginary line that divides Earth into the Northern and Southern Hemispheres). Therefore, storms that hit North America must be at least 500 miles (805 km) north of the equator before the force causes them to spin. The second major feature of hurricanes is powerful thunderstorms. Two-thirds of hurricanes form along an area called the Intertropical Convergence Zone, about 10 to 20 degrees north of the equator. In this zone, cool northeasterly breezes and warm southeasterly winds meet. When the warm and cold winds come into contact, clouds form and thunderstorms occur. The interaction of the winds causes a hurricane to move.

A hurricane consists of several parts. The eye is an area of calm air at the center of the storm. The eye wall is the main part of the hurricane—the area of rain and wind that wraps around the eye. Rain bands are composed of clouds that spin out from the eye wall, making the hurricane bigger and bringing rain to a much larger area. When a hurricane moves across a region, the area is first battered by strong winds and rain. Next, the eye passes over, and there is a

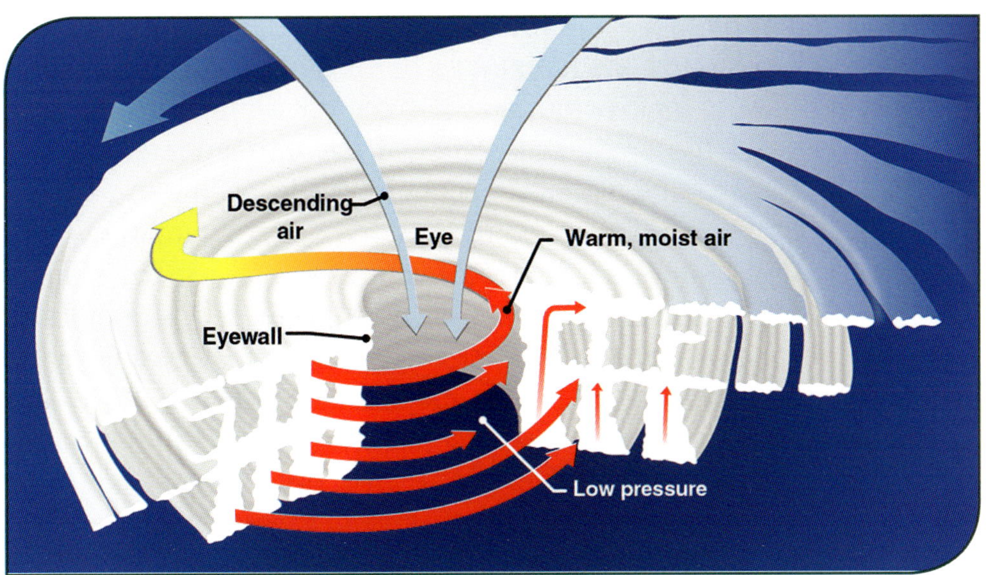

This diagram shows how a hurricane forms as warm moist air (small red arrows) rises and forms bands around the eye, and cold air (blue arrows) sinks.

period of calm. The storm is not over, however. The wind and rain occur again as the other side of the storm passes over the region. Rain bands can allow the rain to continue for some time after the main part of the hurricane has moved on.

Where Hurricanes Strike

Although hurricanes commonly start in the tropics, winds move hurricanes far from the area where they formed. They can move around the Gulf of Mexico through Georgia, Alabama, Mississippi, Louisiana, and Texas. They move east across Florida, or even up the East Coast of the United States as far north as New York and Massachusetts. The air pressure is lower at the bottom of a hurricane than at the top. This difference in pressure causes warm winds to be drawn up into the hurricane and to pass out the top. This process is much like the way fluid is pulled up through a soda straw when a person sucks on it. The thunderstorms were initially formed when the hot air near the surface of warm water hit the colder air higher in the atmosphere. Once a hurricane is spinning, the air above it continually draws in warm air and exhausts it out the top. This action raises the air pressure above the storm and lowers it below, causing a continuous increase in the storm's intensity. For this process to continue, the storm needs moisture. Therefore, whichever direction hurricanes go, they strike mainly along coastal areas, continuing to pick up moisture as they move over the ocean. They do sometimes move from the coast across land. As they move inward, however, they gradually lose strength.

An image of Hurricane Pali, taken from NASA's Terra satellite, shows the storm gathering moisture as it passes over the ocean.

Canada does not experience as many hurricanes as the United States. However, hurricanes do sometimes weaken into storms that seriously damage Canadian cities on the Atlantic Coast as they move northward from the United States. For example, in 2011, post-tropical storm Irene had a brutal impact on the province of Quebec because of massive rain bands. These bands extended from Kingston, Ontario, to Halifax, Nova Scotia. At its height, 70 mile-per-hour (113 kmh) winds battered the area east of Quebec City and 6.7 inches (170 millimeters) of rain fell within a few hours, causing landslides and road collapses.

Global Warming and Hurricanes

Earth's temperature is regulated by a process called the greenhouse effect. Molecules of gases such as carbon dioxide, methane, and nitrous oxide trap the sun's heat, causing Earth's temperature to rise. These gases are called greenhouse gases because they heat Earth in a manner similar to the way the glass walls and roof heat a greenhouse. Earth's surface radiates the sun's heat back into space, where it dissipates. Without this effect, Earth's temperature would average about –30°F (–34.5°C). However, too much of these greenhouse gases in Earth's atmosphere prevents the heat from dissipating into space. This heat raises the temperature of Earth's surface. The increase in heat has a negative effect on the environment. One source of greenhouse gases is the burning of fossil fuels, such as coal, oil, and gasoline. Over the last two hundred years, the amount of greenhouse gases in the atmosphere has increased as a result of human activities. The gases can remain in the atmosphere for decades—or even centuries. The collection of these gases is resulting in an increase of Earth's temperature, a process called global warming. One of the effects of global warming is an increase in severe weather events. Hurricanes are affected by global warming in several ways.

Global warming is causing glaciers and polar ice caps to melt, which results in a rise in sea level. This rise can lead to greater storm surges when hurricanes occur. Global warming also leads to higher moisture content in the air, resulting in more rain and more intense storms. Scientists have created computer models that predict that each 3.6°F (2°C) increase in temperature will result in a 10 to 15 percent increase in rainfall within about 62 miles (100 km) of a hurricane, and hurricane intensity will likely increase 1 to 10 percent as well.

What Happens When a Hurricane Strikes

Hurricanes can cause immense damage. Heavy rainfall causes flooding not only in the areas over which the hurricane passes, but also hundreds of miles from the center of the storm. Once a hurricane makes landfall, or moves from the ocean onto land, often 5 to 10 inches (13–25 centimeters) of rain falls. In the case of large and slow-moving storms, even greater amounts of rain can occur. This

The powerful winds from Hurricane Maria were strong enough to knock down trees when it struck the Caribbean island of Guadeloupe in 2017.

quantity of rain often exceeds the amount of water that the land can absorb and storm drains can hold. The result is flooded streets, vehicles, buildings, and land.

As a hurricane approaches land, the winds from the storm drive water toward the shore. As the eye of the hurricane reaches land, the water is pushed along with it. This rapid increase in the level of water is called a storm surge. In general, stronger hurricanes produce greater storm surges. Storm surges destroy coastlines and wash away buildings and vessels. In addition to the damage resulting from huge waves, storm surges can result in serious flooding.

The winds of a hurricane range from 74 miles per hour (118 kmh) to more than 155 miles per hour (250 kmh). High winds knock down trees and power lines and rip apart structures. With powerful hurricanes, high winds can last as the hurricane moves farther inland. Hurricanes can also spawn tornadoes. Tornadoes are rapidly spinning, funnel-shaped windstorms. They move swiftly across the land and tear up and destroy everything in their path.

A hurricane can destroy millions of dollars' worth of property. Vital infrastructure—such as electrical, phone, and water delivery systems and roads—is damaged. Fragile ecosystems are harmed. People can be stranded, injured, and killed. Scientists and engineers are seeking to develop ways to protect people and property from these storms.

CHAPTER TWO

Storm Watch

Researchers use technology to study the causes and behavior of hurricanes. Having an understanding of hurricanes enables scientists to predict where and when hurricanes are likely to strike. It also helps engineers and city planners to prepare for hurricanes, to design structures that will withstand them, and to reduce their effects.

How Scientists Study Hurricanes

NOAA and the National Hurricane Center (NHC) predict hurricanes and the paths they will take. They also warn people about the danger. This advance warning allows people and authorities to prepare for hurricanes and, if necessary, evacuate an area. Prior to the availability of aircraft to study hurricanes and tropical storms, hurricanes would form and strike without warning. The result was often a very large loss of life.

Forecasting hurricanes is a complex process. Scientists need a great deal of data to make accurate predictions. The National Aeronautics and Space Administration (NASA) plays a key role in providing this data. One set

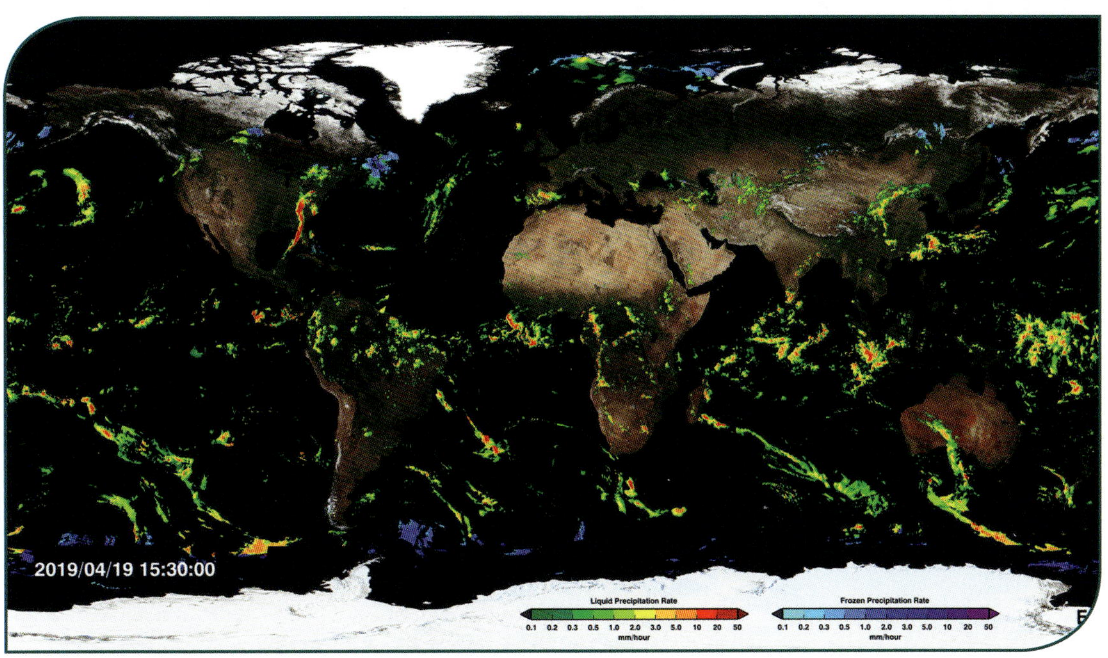

An image from NASA's Global Precipitation Measurement network of satellites shows nearly real-time precipitation around the world.

of tools that NASA uses to provide data on hurricanes consists of satellites that orbit Earth. These weather-related satellites provide information on Earth's atmosphere, land, snow and ice, oceans, and rain, among other factors. The mission of these satellites is to gain knowledge about Earth's climate and climate change. Satellites are also used "to map the effect of human activity and natural disasters on communities and ecosystems," according to NASA. The satellites provide a view of every storm affecting Earth each day, letting scientists watch each one. Among the data collected are rainfall rates, surface wind speed, the height of clouds, the temperature of the oceans, and humidity.

NASA's Global Precipitation Measurement and the NASA/NOAA Suomi National Polar-orbiting Partnership satellites use passive microwave imagers to collect data on where water is churning in clouds during hurricanes. This process works on clouds much like the way an X-ray goes through the human body to provide an image of the structure inside. In 2016, NASA launched the Cyclone Global Navigation Satellite System (CYGNSS), a group of eight small satellites. CYGNSS probes the inner core of hurricanes to provide a better understanding of how they strengthen. CYGNSS can take frequent measurements within storms as they go through their life cycle. It makes accurate measurements of ocean surface winds near and in the eye of the storm. Thus, it can provide more accurate forecasts of hurricanes.

Meteorologists are scientists who study weather. The information obtained from space-based systems helps them to predict where storms are likely to form. It also helps meteorologists forecast where and when storms are likely to become more powerful. In addition, it enables them to predict where and when a hurricane will strike and land as well as its likely strength on impact.

Another tool that scientists use to study hurricanes is computer modeling. Researchers feed the program data on various aspects of the weather at a certain location. They include information such as wind speed, humidity, temperature, and the like. The computer then provides a prediction as to whether a hurricane is likely to occur. It forecasts the hurricane's intensity and the path it is likely to take. One advantage of computer modeling is that researchers can model "what if?" situations. In these models, the scientists use hypothetical values for the various types of data. The results show what would happen if those conditions were to occur. For example, they can observe what the effect on hurricane formation would be if Earth's surface temperature were to rise 3.6°F (2°C). They can also study what would happen if sea level were to rise due to global climate change.

Scientists use aircraft, such as airplanes and helicopters, to carry out field missions to study hurricanes as well. The aircraft can be equipped with a wide range of instruments, including the following:

Radiometer: A device that uses light and a computer program to calculate the wind speed and rain rate in hurricanes and tropical storms in real time.

Dropsonde system: A device dropped over water from an aircraft. The device measures storm conditions as it falls to Earth.

Lidar (Light Detection and Ranging): A system that bounces pulses of light off a target. The light bounces back to a sensor. It is used to measure moisture and winds in a storm.

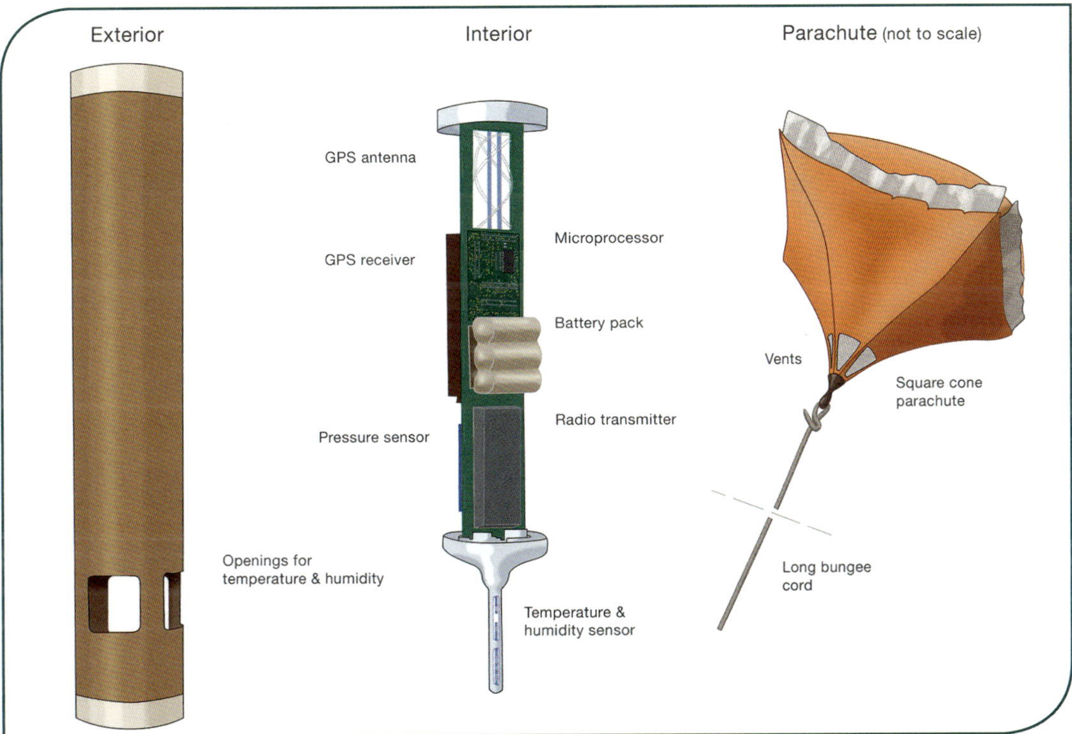

This drawing illustrates the parts of a dropsonde weather device. The device's GPS and weather sensors collect data as the dropsonde falls to Earth after being dropped from an aircraft. The data is sent back to the aircraft via radio transmission.

Doppler radar system: A type of radar used to create a three-dimensional (3D) image of the rain and winds within storms.

These instruments are often used to monitor hurricanes and tropical storms as they evolve.

Categorizing Hurricanes

The Saffir-Simpson Hurricane Wind Scale assigns a hurricane a number from 1 to 5, according to its sustained wind speed. The categories in the scale as given by the National Hurricane Center

Category 1: Winds 74 to 95 miles per hour (119–153 kmh). Buildings could experience damage to elements such as roofs and siding. Branches could break from trees and power lines could come down.

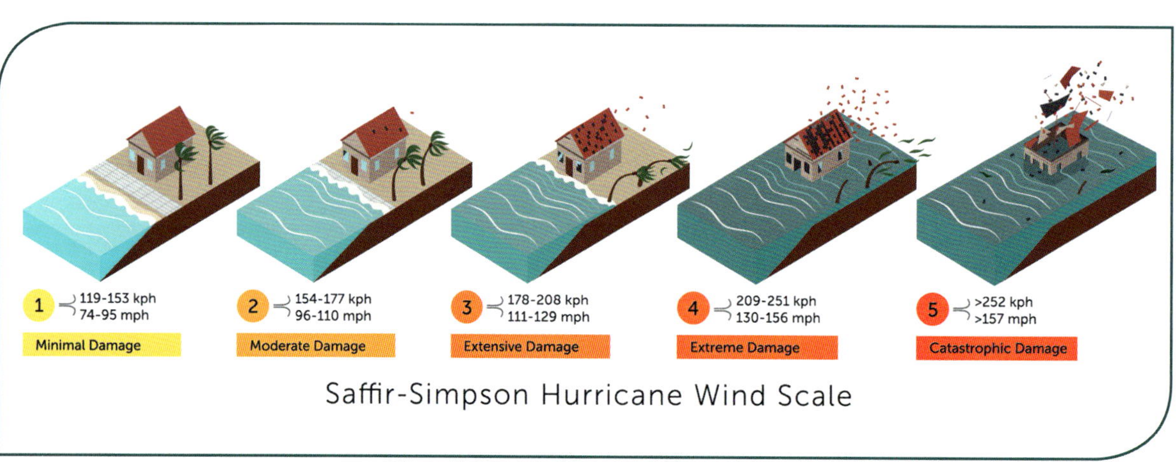

Saffir-Simpson Hurricane Wind Scale

The Saffir-Simpson Hurricane Wind Scale categorizes hurricanes according to the level of damage they may cause.

Category 2: Winds 96 to 110 miles per hour (154–177 kmh). Buildings could experience major roof and siding damage. Trees could be snapped or uprooted, and power outages are common.

Category 3: Winds 111 to 129 miles per hour (178–208 kmh). Buildings are likely to incur major damage, with houses possibly losing roofs and decks. Uprooted trees will block roads, and electricity and water systems will be unavailable because of damage.

Category 4: Winds 130 to 156 miles per hour (209–251 kmh). The exterior walls as well as roofs of buildings will be damaged. Trees will be uprooted and power poles knocked down. Most of the affected area will be uninhabitable for weeks or months after the storm.

Category 5: Winds 157 miles per hour and more (251 kmh). A high percentage of houses will be totally destroyed. Most of the area will be uninhabitable for weeks or months.

Although hurricanes are categorized on the basis of wind strength, their storm surges will destroy vessels, coastal structures, and coastlines. Flooding will cause damage in addition to that caused by wind. The stronger the hurricane, the greater the flood damage. In 2005, Hurricane Katrina caused flooding in New Orleans, Louisiana, that reached a height of 20 feet (6 m) inside some buildings when the levees holding back water around Lake Pontchartrain failed.

Tracking Hurricanes

The World Meteorological Organization (WMO) of the United Nations (UN) has established a series of Regional Specialized Meteorological

The Worst Hurricanes

The following are some of the worst hurricanes to hit the United States in the twentieth and twenty-first centuries, according to the Weather Channel and WIS News, Columbia, South Carolina:

- Galveston hurricane, Texas, 1900: The Galveston hurricane killed almost 8,000 people, according to Weather Channel estimates, and caused about $30 million ($900 million in 2019 dollars) in damage. As reported by NOAA, wind gusts exceeded 135 miles per hour (217 kmh) and a 15-foot (5 m) storm surge covered the entire island, destroying 3,600 buildings and trapping people. The Galveston Hurricane is the deadliest US hurricane ever.

- Lake Okeechobee hurricane, Florida, 1928: 2,500 deaths and $100 million in damage (about $1.5 billion in 2019 dollars) resulted from this hurricane. The storm traveled inland, collapsing the dikes around Lake Okeechobee, releasing floodwaters that drowned thousands in nearby communities.

- Labor Day hurricane, Florida, 1935: Striking the Florida Keys as a category 5 hurricane, it led to 408 deaths and $6 million ($109 million in 2019 dollars) in damage. It is the strongest hurricane to ever hit the United States.

- 1938 hurricane: This storm began on September 15, 1938, east of Puerto Rico and moved up the East Coast to Long Island, New York; Connecticut; and Rhode Island. It had winds over 180 miles per hour (290 kmh) and tides that rose 14 feet (4 m). It killed 256 people and caused $308 million dollars (about $5.5 billion in 2019 dollars) in damage.

- Hurricane Katrina, Louisiana/Mississippi, 2005: Hurricane Katrina caused between 1,200 and 1,800 deaths and $161 billion in damage. It overwhelmed the New Orleans system of levees, causing massive flooding.

- Hurricane Sandy, New York/New Jersey, 2012: Hurricane Sandy led to 147 deaths and $65 billion in damage, mostly due to a huge storm surge that inundated coastal New Jersey and Lower Manhattan.

- Hurricane Harvey, Texas, 2017: Hurricane Harvey caused 89 deaths and $125 billion in damage, largely because the storm sat over the city of Houston for two days.

- Hurricane Irma, Florida, 2017: Irma caused 129 deaths and $50 billion in damage, devastating much of the Caribbean and western Florida.

- Hurricane Maria, Puerto Rico, 2017: Hurricane Maria resulted in 2,975 deaths and $90 billion in damage. It crippled Puerto Rico's infrastructure.

Centers (RSMCs) and Tropical Cyclone Warning Centers (TCWCs). These centers issue tropical cyclone forecasts and warnings for their particular regions. NOAA's National Hurricane Center (NHC) is the agency that forecasts hurricane and tropical storm activity in the Atlantic and Eastern Pacific Oceans around North America. Other agencies that are not part of the UN system also forecast hurricanes. Among these agencies are the US Navy's Joint Typhoon Warning

Center (JTWC), the US Navy's Pacific Meteorology and Oceanography Center, and the Canadian Hurricane Centre. In the United States, hurricane warnings are issued jointly to the public by the NHC and local National Weather Service (NWS) Weather Forecast Offices (WFOs). NWS WFOs provide forecasts before, during, and after a US landfall, including storm surge, wind damage, and inland flooding from rainfall.

The NHC predicts the path, force, size, and structure of hurricanes. It also forecasts their related storm surges, rainfall, and tornadoes. It forecasts the likelihood of a hurricane forming within forty-eight hours. The NHC communicates updated information on hurricanes every six hours.

As noted, the NHC uses data from satellites, aircraft, ships, buoys, and other land-based systems such as radar to track hurricanes and predict their path. The *Global Hawk*, an experimental aircraft

NASA's *Global Hawk* autonomously operated unmanned aircraft is used to monitor and provide information on hurricanes and severe storms.

from NASA, is being tested to examine its capabilities for acquiring hurricane data. After a hurricane makes landfall, automated surface observation stations (ASOSs) and weather balloons take additional measurements.

The data gathered by these various methods are used to create hurricane forecasting models. These models are often called numerical weather prediction (NWP) models. Models result in computer-generated predictions of a hurricane's future track and strength. NHC has a number of different groups involved in the forecasting process. Among these are the Tropical Analysis and Forecast Branch (TAFB), the Hurricane Specialists Unit (HSU), and the Hurricane Liaison Team (HLT). The TAFB provides forecasts for the tropical oceans twenty-four hours each day, year-round. During the hurricane season, the TAFB and the Technical Support Branch (TSB) provide information on hurricanes' location and strength. The HSU keeps a watch on tropical cyclones in the Atlantic and Eastern Pacific basins and analyzes data from various sources. According to HurricaneScience.org, the HSU issues an average of 700 full advisory packages each year to emergency managers and the mass media.

The HLT is a team made up of federal, state, and local emergency managers, Federal Emergency Management Agency (FEMA) personnel, and specially trained National Weather Service (NWS) forecasters. The team functions as a link between NHC and local emergency managers who are charged with addressing a hurricane threat. The HLT communicates information on the progress and threat level of a storm. Then, local and state emergency managers make decisions on how to prepare for the hurricane. They decide how best to protect the community, stage resources, provide information to local media, and, if necessary, order evacuations.

CHAPTER THREE

Making Buildings Safer

Engineers play a key role in developing infrastructure and buildings. They work with city planners to design, build, and rebuild cities. They are also involved in deciding how to locate protective structures in hurricane-prone areas, in relation to environmental features such as wetlands or coasts.

Designing Hurricane-Proof Cities

After a city experiences a major hurricane, city planners try to rebuild the city so it will better withstand storms in the future. Engineers play a pivotal role in this design process.

The island city of Galveston, Texas, provides an example of how a city can be built to minimize damage from hurricanes. From August 27, 1900, to September 17, 1900, a hurricane battered Galveston. The storm surge and winds killed nearly 8,000 of the 40,000 people living there and destroyed more than 3,600 structures on the island, according to NOAA.

Since then, Galveston has weathered other storms, such as Hurricane Harvey, which occurred from August 17, 2017, to September 2, 2017. The reason that the city has continued to survive is that, after the 1900 hurricane, the residents and government authorities rebuilt in specific ways to protect against future hurricanes. Federal, state, and local government authorities cooperated to build a 10-mile-(16 km) long seawall to protect the city from storm surges. Galveston then embarked on an enormous engineering project to raise the whole city above flood level. This effort meant elevating buildings by as much as 16 feet (5 m). Construction workers filled the foundations of buildings with millions of tons of sand to provide them with a new base.

This view shows the seawall that engineers built in Galveston, Texas, to protect against surges from hurricanes.

Like Galveston, Miami and other Florida cities have been devastated by hurricanes and have responded by making changes that make them less vulnerable. In 1992, Hurricane Andrew destroyed entire communities across Florida. A major factor in the storm's destructiveness was that many houses were flimsy. Some roofs were attached with staples instead of nails; some houses were constructed of particle board, not wood. Also, many people lived in mobile homes that were not anchored to the ground. In 2002, the Florida legislature enacted a statewide building code, a set of rules for how buildings are to be constructed. The code requires building materials and methods that enable structures to stand up to winds of 111 miles per hour (179 kmh). In areas likely to be hit by stronger winds, such as Miami-Dade County, buildings must withstand winds of 130 miles per hour (209 kmh).

Stronger construction is only one element of protecting a city. Old drainage systems in many towns and cities are inadequate to deal with the large quantities of water that fall during a hurricane. City governments have to update or replace drainage systems and install new stormwater pumps. The cities also have to elevate buildings and roads. To protect against storm surges, engineers must construct massive seawalls. Water-permeable paving materials allow water to reach the earth beneath them. These new types of surfaces, such as concrete with pores, help prevent roads from flooding and create

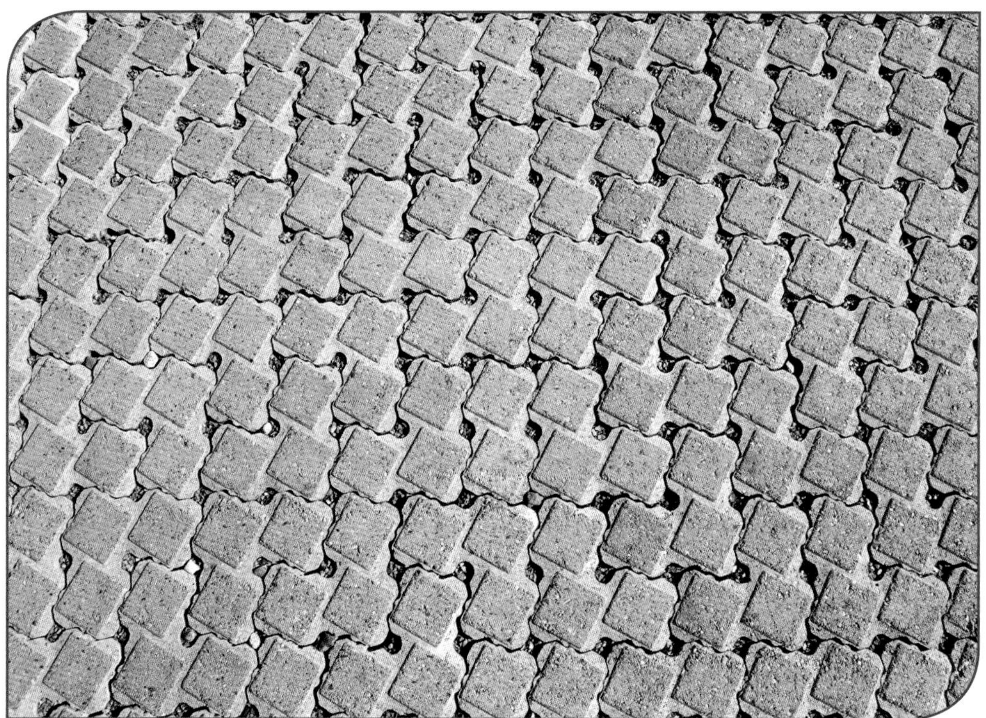

Water-permeable pavers used on roads and driveways help provide drainage for stormwater, reducing flooding in hurricane-prone areas, such as Florida.

more drainage as well. Utilities need to place power lines on metal or concrete poles rather than wooden ones. Guy wires (cable-like supports) anchor the poles to the ground to make them better able to withstand winds.

Using the Environment to Reduce Flooding

People often think of nature as a force to be resisted and focus on using man-made structures to resist the power of hurricanes. However, nature itself can help protect human beings.

In coastal areas, reefs, islands, mangrove swamps, beaches, and dunes provide a buffer against hurricanes and help break up their force. Engineers can encourage their development by, for example, placing sand on a coastline. The ocean currents and waves push the sands inland, creating new and bigger beaches. The natural sediment that collects around dams can be used to create new "islands" in some hurricane-prone areas. These act as storm breaks because hurricanes draw less moisture as they pass over land, which helps reduce their power.

Engineers recommend creating more and larger green spaces in urban areas. They also suggest creating and protecting wetlands (natural areas like marshes, swamps, and bayous that are filled with water). These wetlands provide more drainage. Roads that have two driving lanes and one "green" lane filled with grass rather than asphalt also provide drainage along streets. Researchers also suggest that adding roof gardens to industrial and commercial buildings helps absorb water. Giving water more natural places to drain reduces flooding. All these natural spaces allow the city to absorb large amounts of water and release it slowly over time. The city becomes more like a sponge and less like a bowl.

Hurricane-Proof Buildings

Engineers develop techniques and materials to protect homes and commercial buildings from hurricanes. One of the most critical components of hurricane-proofing buildings is keeping windows intact during a hurricane. If a window breaks in a house, higher-pressure air gets inside, and the pressure can cause the house to blow apart. Builders of new homes in hurricane-prone areas often use windows made of laminated glass that encloses a sheet of Kevlar, a very strong man-made fiber. Hurricane shutters help protect windows from debris that is thrown around by powerful winds. Basic storm shutters are made of plywood, but higher-end homes often have shutters made of metal or polycarbonate plastic.

To prevent flooding from rain and storm surges, especially in areas like Florida and Louisiana, where the land is below sea level, builders place houses on concrete pilings. Pilings are posts driven into the ground to support a structure. The pilings also keep the building from collapsing when shaken by heavy winds. When builders construct new houses in hurricane zones, they install hurricane straps. These are pieces of steel that attach the walls to the rafters, to keep the roof from being blown off. Homeowners can install hurricane straps in existing constructions, but the process is difficult and expensive because the sheetrock walls must be cut to reach the beams, and then repaired.

One aspect of home construction that might not immediately seem critical is the garage door. However, many houses lose their entire roof because the garage door fails and the garage is filled with high-pressure air. Therefore, impact-resistant garage doors are an important part of hurricane-proof residential construction.

Architects and engineers design hurricane-resistant commercial buildings with foundations high enough to raise them above sea level. They use masonry and concrete for the first floor to provide a waterproof barrier that helps protect against flooding. They sometimes use insulated concrete blocks (ICB) to construct buildings. Buildings constructed with this material are much stronger than steel-framed and wood buildings. Using ICB to construct buildings makes them resistant to winds up to 200 miles per hour (322 kmh) and debris flying at speeds up to 100 miles per hour (161 kmh). Architects, builders, and engineers constructing buildings in flood hazard zones must follow the rules in the American Society of Civil Engineers 24

This hurricane-proof, all-metal building under construction in Naples, Florida, is an example of the way engineers are approaching construction to withstand hurricanes.

(ASCE 24) standard in the International Building Code. ASCE 24 requires elevated structures, the use of materials that can safely get wet, and the use of design assemblies that easily dry out after exposure to moisture.

Engineers and architects must design buildings to withstand powerful winds and flying debris. In addition to ICB, structures need to provide a path for wind that directs it away from the roof and walls and toward the foundation. Channeling the wind in this way keeps its pressure on the building steady, which holds the roof, walls, floors, and foundation together. Proper design and construction are the keys to creating buildings that can withstand the power of a hurricane.

CHAPTER FOUR

Surviving the Storm

Individuals need to prepare in advance to remain safe during a hurricane. After a hurricane strikes, people need to repair their property, and municipal authorities must manage recovery activities for the community. Engineers work with authorities to assess and manage hurricane damage.

Be Prepared

Preparation for a hurricane starts before the hurricane season begins. Residents should familiarize themselves with all the evacuation routes in the area so they can quickly comply with instructions to leave. Homeowners need to check their house, or have a home inspector or engineer do so to be sure it will withstand hurricanes. If necessary, improvements should be made so the structure complies with hurricane-zone building codes. Residents need to assemble tools and supplies, including a first aid kit and adequate food and water.

In areas prone to hurricanes, homeowners sometimes choose to have a fuel-powered backup generator that provides electricity when the power goes out. It is best to purchase one well in advance or make sure the existing one is in good repair. It is important to keep an adequate

Hurricane-prone cities use blue signs to clearly mark evacuation routes; residents should note these routes before a storm strikes.

supply of fuel stored safely and to understand how to operate the generator safely before using it. Anyone who uses a medical device that relies on electricity must make sure that there is a backup battery-powered system (uninterruptible power supply) to allow it to continue to operate.

Once a hurricane warning is announced, homeowners need to close storm shutters or fasten sheets of plywood over windows. Since drinkable water may not be available after a hurricane strikes, it is a good idea to store some cases of gallon bottles of filtered or spring water (1 gallon per person for three days). To have water for nondrinking purposes, residents should fill the bathtubs with water before the hurricane strikes. They should store a supply of canned and boxed food. Gas stoves can be used for cooking even when electricity goes out, as long as gas lines in the area are intact. A long fireplace match can be used to light the burner, since only the sparker that lights the flame is electric. The welfare of pets needs to be considered too. Emergency supplies should include pet food and means of securing pets, including leashes and carriers in case they need to go to a shelter with their owner.

Residents need to prepare an interior or cellar room with supplies where they can take shelter during the storm. A weather band or weather alert radio is useful to receive information during the storm because it can pick up the broadcast frequency of the National Weather Service (the NOAA network). It is a good idea to have lots of flashlights and batteries on hand. If authorities recommend evacuation, residents should leave immediately. Those who are stubborn and refuse to leave not only place their lives at risk, but the lives of responders who may have to rescue them after the storm hits.

Residents prepare their home to survive a hurricane and protect the family by covering windows with plywood boards.

It is very dangerous to go outside during the pause when the eye passes over. The backside of the storm will be coming behind it. After the storm, residents need to make sure there is no dangerous debris outside before exiting the building. One should check for downed power lines around the house—but not touch them, which can be fatal. The power company should be contacted immediately to handle them. Power and phone lines may be out and it may take hours, days, or longer to get electrical systems up and running. Therefore, one should make sure to have enough supplies to last for some time after the storm.

Hurricane Preparedness Kit

A hurricane preparedness kit is a knapsack or small suitcase on wheels that residents can keep in a safe room where they can take shelter. An interior room without windows or a finished basement room makes a good safe room. They can quickly grab the kit if they need to leave home at once in case of a hurricane. The following are some items the kit should contain:

- A spare cell phone charger and a portable battery and cable to power a cell phone to make an emergency call
- An LED flashlight and extra batteries
- A weather band or weather alert radio
- A spare pair of eyeglasses
- Commonly used toiletries in travel size, such as toothpaste

and soap or hand sanitizer, tissues, moist hand wipes, roll of toilet paper, hairbrush, and toothbrush

- A first aid kit
- A multipurpose pocket knife or tool with both a blade and a can opener
- A few days' worth of clothing, including a rain poncho
- A lightweight thermal blanket
- A week's supply of medication, including an extra inhaler for asthma if necessary
- Pet food, bowl and extra water, and a leash if appropriate, for any pets
- Sanitary napkins or tampons if necessary
- A paperback book, handheld game, or other entertainment items
- A waterproof bag with photocopies of important documents, including birth certificates, green cards or naturalization certificates, driver's licenses, bank account records (or save these digitally), and proof of insurance; and cash, including some small bills or coins for vending machines
- Bottles of water
- Granola or energy bars

Engineers and Hurricane Recovery Efforts

After a hurricane, engineers play a central role in redesigning cities to withstand future storms. They must design new levees, seawalls, and drainage systems to protect the community from storm surges and flooding. Engineers are employed by city and town authorities to design new solutions for handling flooding, such as deep tunnels, pumping systems, and interbasin transfer systems (which move water from one water storage area to another) to reduce the likelihood of flooding.

Engineers are often included on city and town task forces charged with rebuilding cities to reduce the amount of damage caused by future hurricanes. For example, after Hurricane Harvey in 2017 caused extensive damage to communities in Texas, engineers throughout the state contributed ideas for improved flood risk management, such as the following:

- The establishment of statewide standards to improve flood management
- The use of more stormwater systems
- The creation of a statewide levee safety program
- Expanded funding for dam inspection, maintenance, and improvement

Engineers are employed by local governments to evaluate why buildings and infrastructure fail during hurricanes and to devise ways of rebuilding so that these structures will withstand hurricanes in the future. Engineers must design structures such as buildings, roads,

Engineers assess the damage from a hurricane. After a hurricane, engineers contribute ideas for rebuilding and better withstanding future hurricanes.

and bridges specifically to withstand extreme winds, windborne debris, and flooding. Often, they assist in creating new building codes.

Hurricanes can cause great loss of life and millions of dollars in property damage. Science, technology, engineering, and mathematics (STEM) principles are the basis for better engineering of buildings and infrastructure, such as flood control systems. Improved engineering is the key factor in reducing the cost of hurricanes in terms of lives lost and dollars spent. Engineers use STEM principles to evaluate the requirements for hurricane-proofing a community, develop new strategies and materials, and create designs for better buildings and other structures. They also apply these principles to write standards that ensure that people and property can better survive these extreme storms.

Glossary

automated Something that is run by mechanical, computerized, or robotic equipment.

building code A set of rules that specify how buildings are to be constructed.

Coriolis force A motion-generated force resulting from Earth's rotation.

cyclone A storm that rotates in a counterclockwise direction north of the equator.

diameter The distance across a circle passing through the center from one side to the other.

dissipate To spread out or scatter.

ecosystem All the living and nonliving things in a particular environment.

equator The imaginary line that separates the Earth into the Northern and Southern Hemisphere.

evacuate To leave an unsafe place in an organized way to find protection.

Federal Emergency Management Agency (FEMA) The US government agency responsible for managing the effects of disasters, such as hurricanes.

greenhouse gas A gas such as carbon dioxide, methane, or nitrous oxide that traps the sun's heat in Earth's atmosphere.

guy wire A cable that anchors a structure, such as a power line pole, to the ground.

humidity The amount of moisture in the air.

hypothetical Based on something that seems possible but is not real.

infrastructure The basic systems necessary for a community to function, including electrical, phone, and water systems and roads and transportation systems.

Intertropical Convergence Zone An area 10 to 20 degrees north of the equator where northerly and southerly winds meet, or converge.

Kevlar A high-strength artificial fiber.

mass media Radio and TV stations, newspapers, and other communication outlets that report news to the public.

mitigate To reduce the effects of.

passive microwave imager A device that uses microwaves, a type of energy that works similarly to X-rays, to create an image of the inside of clouds.

permeable Allowing something to pass through.

polycarbonate A type of strong, hard plastic.

predict To foretell something based on what has happened in the past.

radiate To give off rays or shine.

rotation The act of spinning around a central point.

stormwater Water that accumulates from rain.

sustained Continuous or constant.

tropics The area of Earth surrounding the equator.

wetlands Natural areas like marshes, swamps, and bayous that retain water.

For More Information

American Society of Civil Engineers (ASCE)
1801 Alexander Bell Drive
Reston, VA 20191-4400
(800) 548-2723 or (703) 295-6300
Website: https://www.asce.org
Facebook: @ASCEorg
Twitter: @ASCETweets
ASCE develops building standards and works with communities to create hurricane-proof building codes; it offers student memberships, student conferences, and mentoring opportunities.

Environment and Climate Change Canada: Canadian Hurricane Centre (CHC)
Fontaine Building
200 Sacré-Coeur Boulevard
Gatineau, QC K1A 0H3
Canada
(819) 938-3860
Website: https://www.ec.gc.ca/ouragans-hurricanes
Facebook: @EnvironmentandClimateChange
CHC provides current hurricane conditions, storm maps, weather warnings, preparedness information, and a storm tracker.

Federal Emergency Management Agency (FEMA)
500 C Street SW
Washington, DC 20472
(202) 646-2500
Website: https://www.fema.gov
Facebook: @FEMA

Twitter: @Readygov
FEMA is the US government agency that manages the effects of disasters such as hurricanes; it provides preparedness information on its website.

National Aeronautics and Space Administration (NASA)
300 E Street SW, Suite 5R30
Washington, DC 20546
(202) 358-0001
Website: https://www.nasa.gov
Facebook and Twitter: @NASA
NASA operates weather satellites and provides data for scientists studying hurricanes and forecasting storms.

National Oceanic and Atmospheric Administration (NOAA)
National Hurricane Center
11691 SW 17th Street
Miami, FL 33165
(305) 229-4470
Website: https://www.nhc.noaa.gov
Facebook and Twitter: @NWSNHC
YouTube: NOAA/NWS National Hurricane Center
The NOAA National Hurricane Center researches hurricanes, collects data on them, and provides forecasts.

National Weather Service (NWS)
1325 East West Highway
Silver Spring, MD 20910
(800) 992-7433 or (301) 713-0258
Website: https://www.weather.gov
Facebook and Twitter: @NWS
NWS provides up-to-date weather forecasts and information on storms and hurricanes.

For Further Reading

Álvarez Salaverry, Ricardo A. *Hurricane Mitigation for the Built Environment*. Boca Raton, FL: CRC Press, 2016.

Bates, Diane C. *Superstorm Sandy: The Inevitable Destruction and Reconstruction of the Jersey Shore.* New Brunswick, NJ: Rutgers University Press, 2016.

Hoena, B. A. *Hurricane Katrina: An Interactive Modern History Adventure.* North Mankato, MN: Capstone Press, 2014.

Houston Chronicle. *Hurricane Harvey.* Battle Ground, WA: Pediment Publishing, 2017.

Kimber Foundation. *Galveston Seawall Chronicles.* Charleston, SC: The History Press, 2017.

Koontz, Robin. *Define and Design: Disaster-Proof!* North Mankato, MN: Rourke Educational Media, 2017.

Marcias, Courtney Barrett. *Journeys Through Irma: The Hurricane That Made the Keys Community Stronger.* CreateSpace Independent Publishing Platform, 2018.

McCall, Gerri. *Surviving Extreme Weather: How to Survive the Worst Storms, Floods, Droughts and Cold Spells.* London, UK: Amber Books, 2017.

Scibilia, Jade Zora. *Climate Change.* New York, NY: PowerKids Press, 2019.

Shofner, Melissa Raé. *Hammered by Hurricanes*. New York, NY: PowerKids Press, 2018.

Times-Picayune. *Katrina: The Ruin and Recovery of New Orleans.* Updated ed. New Orleans, LA: Times-Picayune, 2007.

Bibliography

Bendix, Aria. "How to Hurricane-Proof Your Home, According to an Architect Who Designs Homes That Could Withstand Category 4 Hurricanes." Business Insider, November 29, 2018. https://www.businessinsider.com/hurricane-proof-home-how-to-2018-11.

Boulter, Sarah, Jean Palutikof, David John Karoly, and Daniela Guitart, eds. *Natural Disasters and Adaptation to Climate Change*. New York, NY: Cambridge University Press, 2018.

Cusick, Daniel. "The Buildings That Survived Michael Hold the Key to Adaptation." *Scientific American*, October 15, 2018. https://www.scientificamerican.com/article/the-buildings-that-survived-michael-hold-the-key-to-adaptation.

Dangerfield, Katie. "Hurricanes in Canada: How Often They Hit and Who Is at Risk." Global News, August 28, 2017. https://globalnews.ca/news/3700345/hurricane-canada-where-storm-will-hit.

Dunlop, Storm. *Meteorology Manual: The Practical Guide to the Weather.* Somerset, UK: Hanes Publishing, 2014.

Geophysical Fluid Dynamics Laboratory. "Global Warming and Hurricanes: An Overview of Research Results." June 6, 2018. https://www.gfdl.noaa.gov/global-warming-and-hurricanes.

HurricaneScience.org. "Hurricane Forecast Regions and Centers." Retrieved February 6, 2019. http://www.hurricanescience.org/science/forecast/forecasting/regionsandcenters.

Hurricaneville.com. "Hurricane Safety Tips." Retrieved February 12, 2019. http://www.hurricaneville.com/safety.html.

Lstiburek, Joseph. "BSD-111: Flood and Hurricane Resistant Buildings." Building Science Corporation, October 6, 2006. https://buildingscience.com/documents/digests/bsd-111-flood-and-hurricane-resistant-buildings.

Mortice, Zach. "Hurricane-Proof Construction Methods Can Prevent the Destruction of Communities." RedShift, November 7, 2017. https://www.autodesk.com/redshift/hurricane-proof-construction-methods-can-save-buildings-communities.

NASA. "How Does NASA Study Hurricanes?" August 14, 2015. https://www.nasa.gov/feature/goddard/how-does-nasa-study-hurricanes.

National Hurricane Center. "Saffir-Simpson Hurricane Wind Scale." Retrieved February 4, 2019. https://www.nhc.noaa.gov/aboutsshws.php.

National Oceanic and Atmospheric Administration. "The Galveston Hurricane of 1900." Revised July 6, 2017. https://oceanservice.noaa.gov/news/features/sep13/galveston.html.

National Oceanic and Atmospheric Administration. "What Is a Hurricane?" Retrieved February 1, 2019. https://oceanservice.noaa.gov/facts/hurricane.html.

Newkirk, Vann R., II. "How to Build Hurricane-Proof Cities." *The Atlantic*, September 12, 2017. https://www.theatlantic.com/politics/archive/2017/09/how-to-build-hurricane-proof-cities/539319.

Office of Coastal Management. "Fast Facts: Hurricane Costs." National Oceanic and Atmospheric Administration. Retrieved February 27, 2019. https://www.coast.noaa.gov/states/fast-facts/hurricane-costs.html.

Peters, Adele. "Four Smart Designs for New Cities That Can Withstand Any Storm." FastCompany, January 7, 2014. https://www.fastcompany.com/3024389/4-smart-designs-for-new-cities-that-can-withstand-any-storm.

Raymond, Jonathan. "From Katrina to Galveston: The Worst Hurricanes to Hit the U.S." WIS News, September 13, 2018. http://www.wistv.com/story/39081309/from-katrina-to-galveston-the-worst-hurricanes-to-hit-the-us.

Roggema, Rob. "Designing Cities to Withstand Natural Disasters." Phys.org, March 30, 2017. https://phys.org/news/2017-03-cities-natural-disasters.html.

Sears, Kathleen. *Weather 101: From Doppler Radar and Long-Range Forecasts to the Polar Vortex and Climate Change, Everything You Need to Know about the Study of Weather*. Avon, MA: Adams Media, 2017.

UCAR Center for Science Education. "The Greenhouse Effect." Retrieved February 2, 2019. https://scied.ucar.edu/longcontent/greenhouse-effect.

University of Rhode Island Graduate School of Oceanography. "National Hurricane Center Forecast Process." Hurricanes: Science and Society. Retrieved March 26, 2019. http://www.hurricanescience.org/science/forecast/forecasting/forecastprocess.

Weather Channel. "Hurricane Damages and Effects." July 8, 2013. https://weather.com/safety/hurricane/news/hurricane-damages-effects-20120330.

Weather Channel. "The 10 Worst Hurricanes in History." Hurricane Central, August 18, 2014. https://weather.com/storms/hurricane/news/10-worst-hurricanes-american-history-20140818#/11.

Index

About the Author

Jeri Freedman earned a BA degree from Harvard University. For more than fifteen years, she worked for companies producing scientific equipment and performing environmental testing. She has written numerous books for young adults, including *Climate Change: Human Effects on the Nitrogen Cycle; The Rising Seas; and Land Formation—The Shifting, Moving Changing Earth: Mountains*. Her house in New Orleans, Louisiana, was damaged during Hurricane Katrina.

Photo Credits

Cover The Washington Post/Getty Images; cover hexagons (left to right) Nattapong Wongloungud/EyeEm/Getty Images, CHUYN/E+/Getty Images, D-Keine/E+/Getty Images, © iStockphoto.com/Alessandro Rizzo, john finney photography/Moment/Getty Images, Fernando Ojeda/EyeEm/Getty Images; pp. 4–5 (background) Warchi/iStock/Getty Images; p. 5 (inset) Pool/AFP/Getty Images; p. 7 Joe Raedle/Getty Images; pp. 9, 10, 15, 22 NASA; p. 12 Cedrick Isham Calvados/AFP/Getty Images; p. 17 Monica Schroeder/Science Source; p. 18 Captain Cobi/Shutterstock.com; p. 25 Stephanie Sellers/Alamy Stock Photo; p. 26 TMI/Alamy Stock Photo; p. 29 dmac/Alamy Stock Photo; p. 32 goodmoments/iStock/Getty Images; p. 33 Logan Cyrus/AFP/Getty Images; p. 37 Robert Nickelsberg/Getty Images; cover and interior pages graphic elements © iStockphoto.com/koto_feja (spiral design), Ralf Hiemisch/Getty Images (dot pattern).

Design and Layout: Tahara Anderson; Senior Editor: Kathy Kuhtz Campbell; Photo Researcher: Sherri Jackson